Peter Rabbit

STICKER STORIES
PETER'S FAVORITE PLACES

I love EXPLORING! Will you come, too?
Add stickers to the scenes as we go.

Let's hop to it!

MAP OF MY WOODS

Here's a map of where I live. It's in my dad's journal, which I always have with me. Add stickers to see who we might meet – my best friends and my WORST enemies!

ROCKY ISLAND

Old Brown
A VERY grumpy owl.

OLD BROWN'S ISLAND

MR. JEREMY FISHER'S POND

SQUIRREL NUTKIN'S WOOD

MRS. TIGGY-WINKLE'S LAUNDRY

Benjamin Bunny
My cousin tries to be brave.

Squirrel Nutkin
Our nuttiest friend.

Cotton-tail
My littlest sister.

Mr. Tod
Foxes eat rabbits.
Need I say more?

JEMIMA PUDDLE-DUCK'S
HILLTOP FARM

MR. MCGREGOR'S
GARDEN

MR. TOD & TOMMY
BROCK'S WOOD

MY BURROW

DR. & MRS. BOBTAIL'S
BURROW

TUNNEL
NETWORK

MR. BOUNCER'S BURROW
(BENJAMIN'S HOME)

Jemima Puddle-duck
A dizzy duck.

Lily Bobtail
My clever friend.

My mom
Mrs. Rabbit to you.

Flopsy and Mopsy
My twin sisters.

HOME SWEET HOME!

This is where I live with my mom and sisters. Mom's a GREAT cook, and we all help her keep our cozy burrow spick-and-span.

MY WOODS

I know these woods like the back of my paw.
Let's have a look around! My BEST friends
Lily and Benjamin are coming, too.

Add stickers to make a trail for Benjamin and Lily to follow.

TREETOP HIDEAWAY

This is our secret clubhouse where we plan the most TIP-TOP adventures. We'll probably bump into Squirrel Nutkin. He always has the nuttiest ideas!

What are the cheeky squirrels playing with?

MR. TOD'S DEN

This is Mr. Tod's house. He'd love to eat us, but we always outfox that sneaky fox. Uh-oh, here he comes . . .

Quick! Add stickers to hide us!

MR. McGREGOR'S GARDEN

We're not supposed to come in here, but the strawberries are so JUICY and the radishes are so CRUNCHY we can't stay away!

Can you add lots of yummy garden goodies?

PARTY AT HILLTOP FARM

So now you've been EVERYWHERE,
but you haven't met EVERYONE.
They'll all be at the summer party . . .

Put up more decorations and choose party food.

CONGRATULATIONS!

SKILL IN EXPLORING CERTIFICATE

Awarded to

Maria White

Age

9

Peter Rabbit
- - - - - - - - - - - - - - - -
PETER RABBIT
CHIEF EXPLORER

Come exploring
with us again soon!

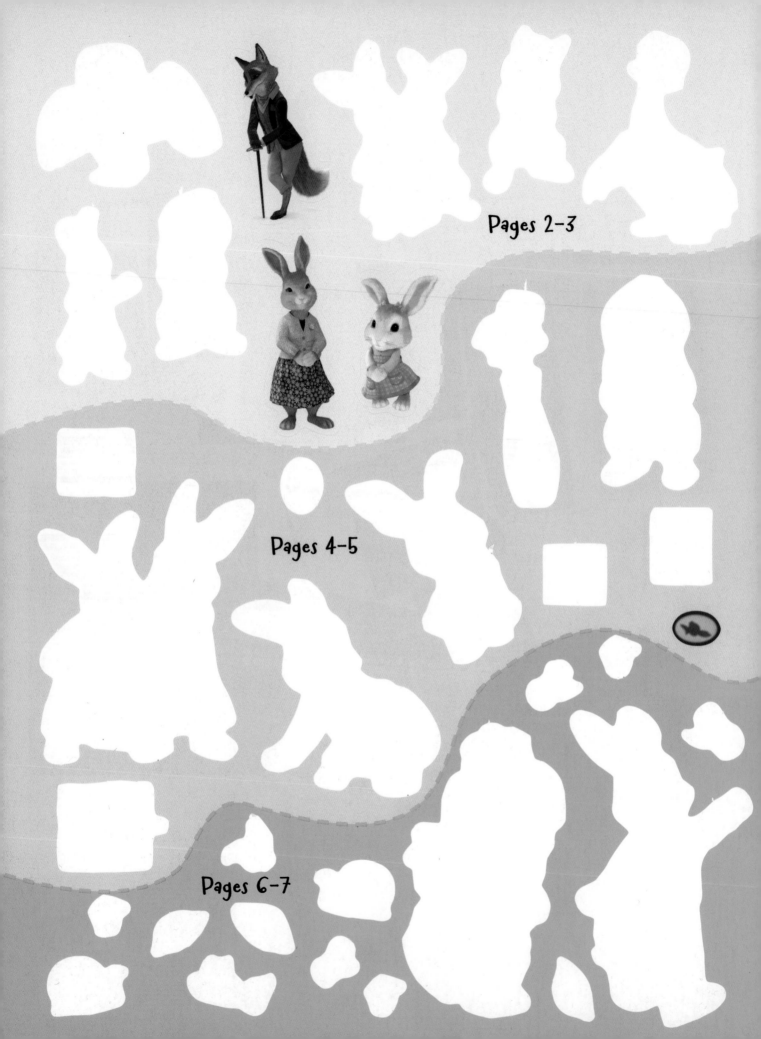

Pages 2-3

Pages 4-5

Pages 6-7

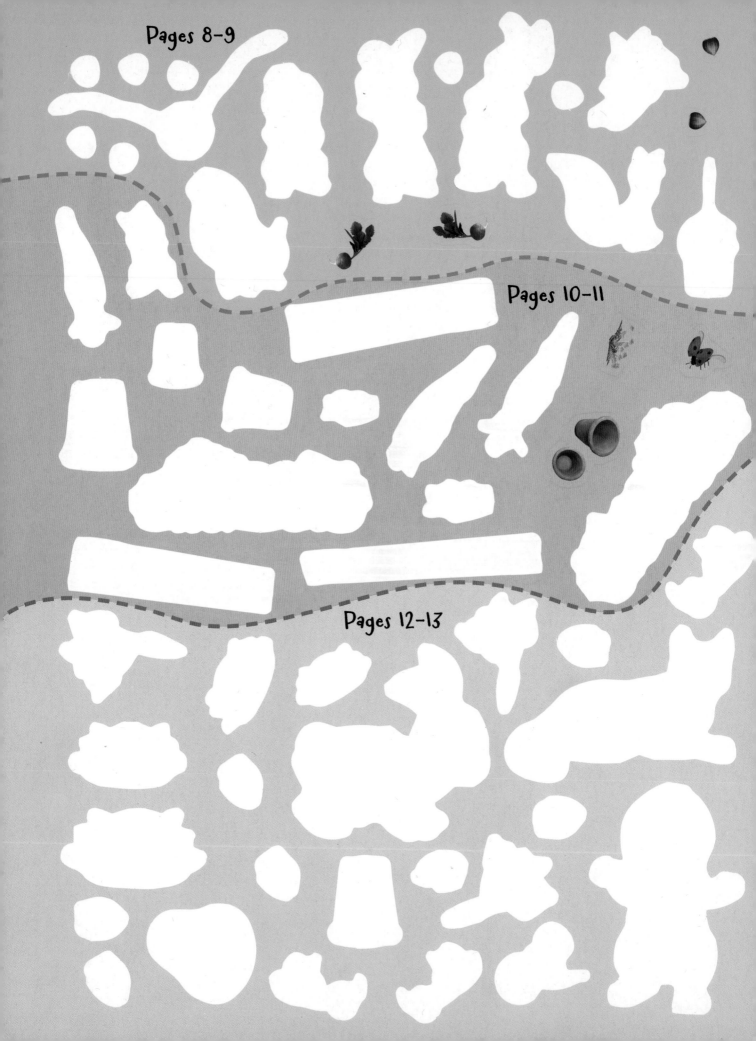

Pages 8-9

Pages 10-11

Pages 12-13